To:

From:

How to Catch a to Reindeer

From the New York Times Bestselling Series

Alice Walstead &
Andy Elkerton

sourcebooks
wonderland

It's Christmas Eve! That's right, Santa's back!
He's here with the whole REINDEER team.
There are presents and stockings and candy canes,
and Christmas trees all agleam.

You might have sung my name before.
The tune starts with Dasher and Dancer!
Next in the song are Prancer and Vixen,
but who's next? Do you know the answer?

Bingo! That's right, I'm *COMET* herself!
I've been with the team from the start.
Christmas is my most favorite thing!
Each Christmas Eve fills my heart.

Now I've already seen the shelf with the elf
and that blue truck loaded with trees.
I've even seen a green Santa so mean!
Tonight, I'll explore as I please.

I've heard that some kids are setting up traps
to catch an elf or maybe Santa Claus.
If you think offering some carrots will work,
I promise I won't even pause.

I'll admit that this trap looks interesting.
It has lights and style and **flair**.
The thing is though, I'm not hungry enough.
There's no way I'm going in there!

FREE

REINDEER
MOSS
INSIDE!

Christmas decorations are awesome and bright!
Those candy canes twinkle and glow.

Though a maze looks like fun, I think that I'll pass,
and I'll romp and play in the snow!

FOR COMET

CANDY CANE MAZE

Why would I need night vision goggles?
My eyes do not need that support.
I think I'll stick with a snowball fight.
That last toss made Blitzen snort!

When did all those new reindeer get here?
I'm surprised, but I must be **BRAVE**!
Is that Santa sitting in a sleigh on the ground?
This is weird... And why won't he wave?

I'm chatting away, but it seems they're not listening.
It's like they don't know that it's me.

Oh wait, I get it! They're just **plastic**!
I'm embarrassed, and hope Prancer didn't see.

What in the holly jolly is that?
Those huge ornaments started moving!
They're rolling and rocking and bouncing around,
I could run, but I want to start grooving!

Whoa-ho-ho!! This is fun and better than a run.

Spin left, swing right! I'm dancing on air!

And a tree with lights to go ROCKIN' around?

Vixen, let's dance as a reindeer pair!

Hey friends, come on over! It's for Reindeergram.
Now let's say Merry Christmas and **flash** a smile!
This was a great stop but a few million to go
Christmas Eve must continue with style!

Back to the roof, Santa's back in the sleigh.
We shouldn't keep the big guy waiting!
In the blink of an eye, we'll take off in the sky.
"On now," Santa calls, "no hesitating!"

I had the most fun ever, to be clear.
I'll see you again–let's do this next year!

Merry Christmas
to all and to all a good night!

True Facts About Reindeer

- Reindeer have night vision.

- They live in the tundra, where they have friends like the arctic bunny.

- Reindeer love to eat moss and lichens, a type of plant that grows on trees and rocks.

- Santa's reindeer can fly, but all reindeer can run up to 50 mph.

Copyright © 2022 by Sourcebooks
Text by Alice Walstead
Illustrations by Andy Elkerton and Sarah Mensinga
Cover and internal design © 2022 by Sourcebooks

Sourcebooks and the colophon are registered trademarks of Sourcebooks.

The art was first sketched, then painted digitally in Photoshop with a Wacom Cintiq tablet.

Published by Sourcebooks Wonderland, an imprint of Sourcebooks Kids
P.O. Box 4410, Naperville, Illinois 60567–4410
(630) 961-3900
sourcebookskids.com

Cataloging-in-Publication Data is on file with the Library of Congress.

Source of Production: Worzalla, Stevens Point, Wisconsin, United States of America
Date of Production: August 2022
Run Number: 5027172

Printed and bound in the United States of America.
WOZ 10 9 8 7 6 5 4 3 2 1